19,506

E
S

Sabin, Louis

The Magic String

The Magic String

Written by Francene Sabin

Illustrated by Joel Snyder

Troll Associates

Library of Congress Cataloging in Publication Data

Sabin, Francene.
   The magic string.

    Summary: Doris uses her magic string to help one of
her ducklings learn to swim.
    [1. Ducks—Fiction. 2. Swimming—Fiction]
I. Snyder, Joel. II. Title.
PZ7.S1172Mag   [E]   81-4076
ISBN 0-89375-547-8   AACR2
ISBN 0-89375-548-6 (pbk.)

Doris has four baby ducks.
They are ducklings.

Doris shows them how to swim.

Three can swim.

Only Dennis cannot swim.

"Do what I do," says Doris.

Dennis tries to swim like Doris.

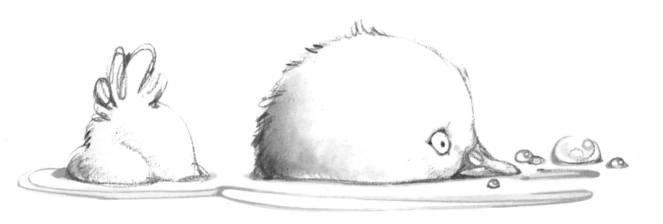

Dennis starts to sink.

Doris pulls Dennis out of the water.

Dennis sits on the grass.

The other ducklings swim by.

Doris takes Dennis into the water.

"Paddle your feet. Flap your wings."

Dennis paddles. Dennis flaps.

Dennis starts to sink again.

"Look. I have a magic string," says Doris.

"What does it do?" asks Dennis.

"It makes ducklings swim," says Doris.

Dennis swims.

Doris smiles. She swims away.

Dennis flaps his wings. The string
comes off.

Dennis swims around the pond.

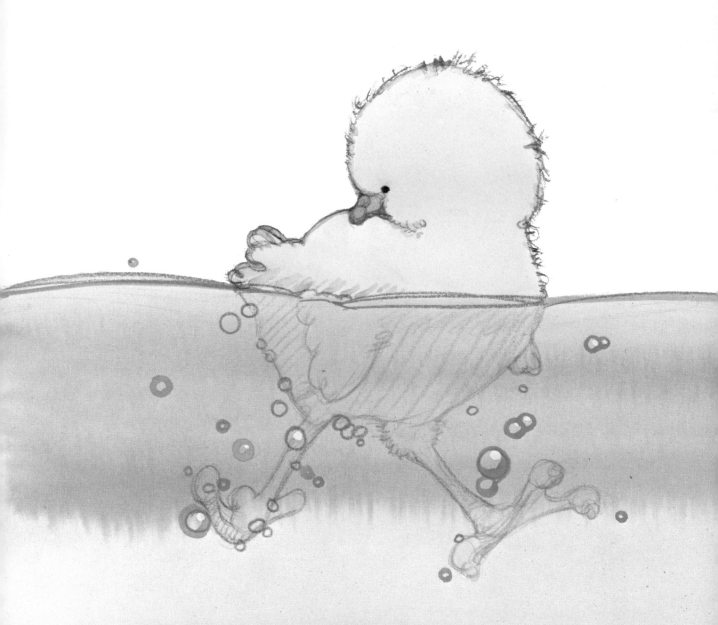

Dennis sees the string is gone.

Dennis starts to sink.

"The string is not magic," says Doris.
"You can swim."

"Yes, you can," say the other ducklings.

Dennis smiles. "Of course I can," he
says.

"I can swim."

A Giant First-Start Reader

This easy reader contains only 73 different words, repeated often to help the young reader develop word recognition and interest in reading.

Basic word list for *The Magic String*

a	has	says
again	have	sees
are	he	she
around	his	shows
asks	how	sink
away	I	sits
baby	into	smiles
by	is	starts
can	it	string
cannot	like	swim
comes	look	swims
course	magic	takes
Dennis	makes	the
do	not	them
does	of	they
Doris	off	three
ducklings	on	to
ducks	only	tries
feet	other	water
flap	out	what
flaps	paddle	wings
four	paddles	yes
gone	pond	you
grass	pulls	your
	say	